EVANSTON PUBLIC LIBRARY
P9-DGF-724

# My Uncle Emily

Philomel Books

JANE YOLEN

Illustrated by
NANCY CARPENTER

# My Uncle Emily

*Special thanks to Prof. Connie Ann Kirk of Mansfield University in Pennsylvania, Jane Wald of the Emily Dickinson Museum, Barbara Diamond Goldin, and Corinne Demas. And my editor Pat Gauch.*

PATRICIA LEE GAUCH, EDITOR

PHILOMEL BOOKS
A division of Penguin Young Readers Group.
Published by The Penguin Group.
Penguin Group (USA) Inc., 375 Hudson Street, New York, NY 10014, U.S.A.
Penguin Group (Canada), 90 Eglinton Avenue East, Suite 700, Toronto, Ontario M4P 2Y3, Canada (a division of Pearson Penguin Canada Inc.).
Penguin Books Ltd, 80 Strand, London WC2R 0RL, England.
Penguin Ireland, 25 St. Stephen's Green, Dublin 2, Ireland (a division of Penguin Books Ltd).
Penguin Group (Australia), 250 Camberwell Road, Camberwell, Victoria 3124, Australia (a division of Pearson Australia Group Pty Ltd).
Penguin Books India Pvt Ltd, 11 Community Centre, Panchsheel Park, New Delhi - 110 017, India.
Penguin Group (NZ), 67 Apollo Drive, Rosedale, North Shore 0632, New Zealand (a division of Pearson New Zealand Ltd).
Penguin Books (South Africa) (Pty) Ltd, 24 Sturdee Avenue, Rosebank, Johannesburg 2196, South Africa.
Penguin Books Ltd, Registered Offices: 80 Strand, London WC2R 0RL, England.


Published simultaneously in Canada. Manufactured in China by South China Printing Co. Ltd.
Design by Semadar Megged. Text set in 17-point MrsEaves. The illustrations are rendered in pen and ink and digital media.
Library of Congress Cataloging-in-Publication Data
Yolen, Jane. My Uncle Emily / Jane Yolen ; illustrated by Nancy Carpenter. p. cm.
Summary: In 1881 Amherst, Massachusetts, six-year-old Gilbert finds it both challenging and wonderful to spend time with his aunt, the reclusive poet Emily Dickinson, who lives next door. 1. Dickinson, Emily, 1830–1886—Juvenile fiction.
[1. Dickinson, Emily, 1830–1886—Fiction. 2. Poets—Fiction. 3. Family life—Massachusetts—Fiction.
4. Amherst (Mass.)—History—19th century—Fiction.] I. Carpenter, Nancy, ill. II. Title. PZ7.Y78My 2009 [E]—dc22 2008032614

ISBN 978-0-399-24005-8
1 3 5 7 9 10 8 6 4 2

To Heidi and Maddison Jane
who both love Emily Dickinson and her poems.
—JY

For Victoria, who, like Emily Dickinson,
is devoted to her flower garden.
—NC

One day when we were in the garden,
choosing flowers for the table,
my Uncle Emily gave me a dead bee
and a poem for my teacher.
Sometimes Uncle Emily is like that,

as if she wants me to see the world
one small bee
and one small poem
at a time.
She calls herself uncle, though she is really my aunt.
She is not at all like an uncle,
for she wears long white dresses
and never smokes cigars.
The "uncle" is a joke in our family.
As for the bee,
it's only between the two of us,
Uncle Emily and me.

I picked an aster and gave it to her.
"In payment for the poem," I said.
She laughed, and in the sun
her hair seemed red and shiny
as a ladybug's shell,
though usually it's brown as a chestnut burr.
"An aster for the poem and not for the bee?" she asked.

We laughed together again, as if at some great joke.
Uncle Emily and I often laugh together
about things we two find funny.
Things like flies in the cupola,
frogs in bogs,
and butterflies, which we call flutter-bys.
But the poem she gave me
was not a joke at all.
Uncle Emily never jokes about poetry,
or about poets, who she says light lamps.

I took the bee and poem into the house.
In the quiet of my bedroom
I read what Uncle Emily had written.
It was in pencil
with not a word crossed out:

*The Bumble Bee's Religion—*

*His little Hearse-like Figure*
*Unto itself a Dirge*
*To a delusive Lilac . . .*

I had so many questions!
Do bumblebees have religion?
Do they pray to flowers?
Do they ride in hearses?

I did not want to take the poem to school,
fearing the boys would not understand it,
fearing that they might laugh at it.
Not laugh in a good way,
as Uncle Emily and I do,
but in a nasty way.
I feared that someone bigger than me
might say something mean about the poem
or about Uncle Emily with a snigger.

But Mother said I must take the poem to school,
for Uncle Emily had written across the top,
"For Gilbert to carry to his Teacher."
"Besides, it is not often that Emily Dickinson
sends a poem out into the world," said Mother.

So I took the poem to Mrs. Howland, my teacher,
who read it to the class and held up the dead bee.
There was a long silence.
No one laughed.

But no one understood the poem either! Not one!
Samuel asked, "Is a bee important enough to be in a poem?"
Thomas called out, "Would a bee have to kneel to pray?"
And Margaret said, "Do bees have knees?"
I could feel my cheeks grow red.

Then at recess, Jonathan,
who is much bigger than me,
called Uncle Emily a name . . . in a very loud voice
that carried across the playing field.
He said, "She is a peculiar old maid and
a reckless . . ."

Reckless! All the boys laughed, but
I stopped Jonathan right there,
stepping up and hitting him for those words.
I had to.
He hit me back, and I fell, twisting my ankle.

But now he had a big red rose
blossoming on his nose.
I told him so and laughed as I said it.
Uncle Emily would not have liked me hitting him,
but she would have liked
"a big red rose blossoming on his nose."
It was almost a poem!

"Thomas Gilbert Dickinson . . ."
Mrs. Howland began, her face an awful worry,
"of all my pupils, that you should fight!"
I had to stand in the corner, wearing a dunce's cap,
as did Jonathan.
I did not care.
I love Uncle Emily
and will not hear her called names.

Then everyone in the class
had to write a thank-you note
to Miss Emily Dickinson for the poem.
Jonathan's thank-you note was in rhyme,
which Mrs. Howland praised.
I thought it peculiar,
but good, too,
like one of Uncle Emily's poems,
and it made me almost forgive him.

My brother Ned came from the town college
to walk me home from school.
He saw that I limped and asked why.
When I told him, he nodded,
and carried me on his back.
"Jonathan meant a *recluse,* not a *reckless,* Gib,
the first being a person
who cannot stand company,
and the other someone who impulsively
punches people in the nose," he said.

So, impulsively I beat on the top of Ned's hat
until he laughed and called out for me to stop.
"Besides," he reminded me,
"Uncle Emily often lowers down
gingerbread in a basket
from her bedroom window
for the neighborhood children,
so she is not entirely a recluse at all.
If you had said that to Jonathan,
it would have put the lie to him,
without a fist being raised."
I nodded and rubbed my hand against his cheek.

I thought him right.
I would not want to hurt the person I love best
in all the world. I would not.
Uncle Emily is the kindest creature.
She would not hurt even a fly,
which she calls her "speck piano."
That is something else I do not understand.
Flies have only a buzz, not piano keys.
But sometimes, if I listen very carefully,
the fly almost seems to make music.
What an idea! I light up with it, like a lamp.
Maybe that is what Uncle Emily means
when she talks about poetry.

So I said not a word all afternoon
about why I was limping.
Not to Mother or Father or Mattie.
Not to Cook either.
I did my chores that day
but could not help limping.
I worried that I would be asked,
and if I told what happened,
it would make Uncle Emily cry
that I had hurt someone on her behalf.
But no one noticed anything.
Grown-ups rarely do.

That evening we went next door to visit.
Uncle Emily cut slices
from her famous black cake.
Aunt Vinnie and my sister, Mattie,
passed the plates around.
When I went up for a second helping,
Uncle Emily saw me limp and asked
about it, for she notices everything.
Poets do that, you know.
I glanced at Ned and he whispered,
"Tell her—but carefully."
So I told about bringing the poem,
and about falling down in the yard after.
But I did not mention what Jonathan said,
or the red rose on his nose,
or the dunce's cap I had to wear all day.
I handed Uncle Emily the thank-you notes.
She liked Jonathan's poem.

Everyone said, "Dear, dear."
Mother cried, "How brave you are when hurt."
Aunt Vinnie added, "And a hero for not crying."
Sister Mattie gave me a hug.
Father said, "You are a man, Gilbert, though you are only six."
Ned just grinned.
But Uncle Emily put her hand to her mouth and cried out, "Dear Gib, I know you well.
Isn't there more to this story?"
And everyone asked, "More?"

They all turned to stare at me,
who had a moment before
been so brave, a hero,
and was now . . . somehow . . . something else.
I ran out into the garden to sob amid the asters.
Not five minutes later Uncle Emily found me,
an old envelope in her hand.
She thrust it at me.
On the back was a poem of hers
I had never heard before.
"Tell all the Truth," it began, "but tell it slant—
Success in Circuit lies."

I read the poem aloud.
No lamps lit in my brain.
"Do you mean that I should tell the story . . ."
"The whole story," she explained,
"with a certain care, so that
the tale comes around to the truth at last."

We tracked into the house, hand in hand.
I looked up at Uncle Emily.
She looked down at me,
with a smile like a Christmas wreath.
"There's something else . . ." I began.
Everyone gaped. "Some few things I forgot to say."

So I dazzled everyone with the full story,
telling the whole truth,
but coming around to it slowly, till the last,
when I said, "Even Jonathan agreed
that a great poet needs thanking,
which he did by trying to write his thanks
in rhyme."

I ended by reading Uncle Emily's poem,
with great gusto and understanding.
Everyone clapped. But the applause
was not half as warming
as my Uncle Emily's smile.

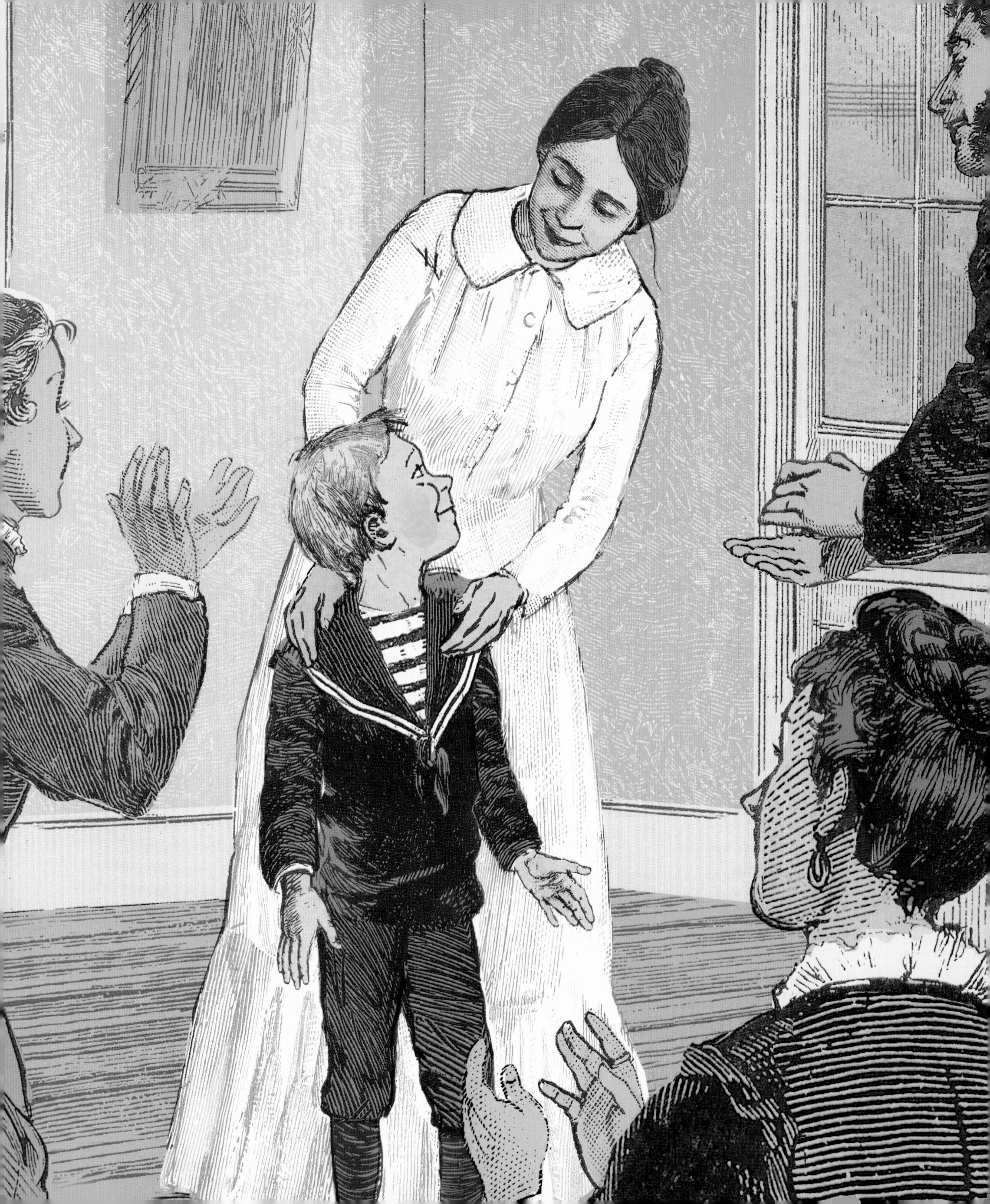

## What Is True About This Story

Emily Dickinson of Amherst, Massachusetts, always wore long white dresses, she was reclusive except within her family and with a few of the neighborhood children, and she positively doted on her nephews and niece. Often she scribbled poems on the backs of old envelopes. At the time of this story, she and her younger sister, Lavinia (Vinnie), dwelt with their mother, who had had a stroke that left her without speech and had a broken hip that kept her bedridden in the Dickinsons' house, known as The Homestead. Next door in The Evergreens were her brother, Austin, his wife Susan, and their three children—Ned, Mattie, and Gib.

Emily really did give the dead bee and poem to six-year-old Thomas Gilbert (called Gib) to take to his teacher sometime in 1881, as reported in a letter. In fact bumblebees were a special token between them. The charmed Emily had written of Gib when he was just a toddler, "Austin's Baby says when surprised by statements—'There's—sumthn—else—there's Bumbul Beese.'" Of Ned she wrote, "He inherits his Uncle Emily's ardor for the lie."

Whether any boy in Mrs. Howland's school on Prospect Street would have dared call Emily Dickinson names, I don't know. But certainly if one had, the adoring Gib would have defended her honor.

Alas, Gib lived only two years beyond the time he took the letter and bee to school, dying of typhoid in 1883. Emily wrote: "I see him in the Stars, and meet his sweet velocity in everything that flies." Ned—who suffered with epilepsy—died in his late thirties. Mattie married and lived a long life, dying in 1943. She had no children.

The complete "Tell all the Truth" poem is:

Tell all the Truth but tell it slant—
Success in Circuit lies
Too bright for our infirm Delight
The Truth's superb surprise
As Lightning to the Children eased
With explanation kind
The Truth must dazzle gradually
Or every man be blind.